# Jude
## and the
# Giant
### of
# Pittenweem

*Nannie McLeod*

© Nanzie McLeod 2008

First published in the United Kingdom by
Nanzie McLeod, Glasgow

The author has asserted her moral rights.

British Library Cataloguing-in Publication Data.
A catalogue record for this book is available from
the British Library.

ISBN 0 9529527 5 0

Origination and design by Robographics, Glasgow
Printed by Bell & Bain Limited, Glasgow

*Also by Nanzie McLeod*

Tales of the Arlington

●

Tales of the East Neuk

●

Pittenweem Sojourn

●

I Never Could Do Crosswords

●

Girl In a Pink Hat

• T H A N K S •


    I want to thank Esther and Jude Mcleod and also Derek Burr for modelling for the illustrations in this book and I am very grateful to Jules Duncan for his helpful research. Thanks also to my daughters Kate Airlie and Sarah McLeod for their helpful suggestions and encouragement.

*The front cover painting
and all of the illustrations
throughout this book
were created by the author,
Nanzie McLeod.*

# List of Illustrations

In a house in the High Street, a little boy stayed.

Jude was courageous and never afraid,
    when his Mum told him stories of long ago things,

Dinosaurs, dragons and horses with wings,

Witches, hobgoblins and singing frogs, sea serpents and
    mermaids and saucer-eyed dogs.

He listened enthralled to each scary tale and never once
    trembled and never turned pale.

He wanted to think that it was all so,

But he shook his head and said "I don't know"

For he could not believe that these stories were true.

Nor can I quite believe it!

What about you?

But Esther, his Mum, said "You never can tell.

We might just discover a magic spell!

For Pittenweem is a magical town,
    with wynds going up and wynds going down

And fishing boats sailing off to catch fish.

I promise to try and grant you a wish?"

Esther and Jude walked down the West Wynd,

Going to see what they could find on the beach,
amongst stones and shells, to make some
magic and cast some spells.

As they walked down that curving wynd, it was
only Jude who looked behind,

For he heard a funny snoring sound that seemed
to come from all around.

And there! Sticking up behind a wall,

Were two feet belonging to somebody TALL,

Two BIG bare feet, with ten HUGE toes.

An ENORMOUS person was having a doze,

Gently sleeping, enjoying his dream,

In that flower filled garden in Pittenweem.

Jude could not believe it was just as it seemed.

Perhaps he was dazzled by sunrays that gleamed.

To his Mum, he said not a single word,

Afraid she'd reply "That's quite absurd!"

"Now for enchantment!" Esther said,
"I'm going to conjure a real mermaid.
I"ll make her so REAL that people will stare,
And I think I'll use seaweed for her hair.
I used to make magic when I was small.
Let's hope I've not forgotten it all.
We'll put seven pebbles in a row,
Then twenty limpet shells, just so...
Now push fourteen sticks into the sand..."

But Jude was watching a massive HAND
    that rested on a nearby roof

Here was REAL magic! Here was PROOF!

Though a lesser boy might shake with fright,
    our Jude smiled and shivered with delight.

"Put on your coat, dear if you're feeling cold"

"Oh no, not a bit, Mum, I'm feeling BOLD!"

But he said not a word about what was in view,

For his Mum might be frightened and get in a stew.

And things are not always just as they seem.

Perhaps this was just a daytime dream.

Thursday was civic amenity day,

When all the recycling was put away.

Glass, plastic and paper were stowed in the car,

Then they drove to the dump, which was not too far.

At first Jude helped Mum like a dutiful boy,

But it was not a task to bring much joy,

For there really was an awful lot.

And soon he wandered from the spot.

Down to the burn, where it smelled damp and green,

And strange plants, birds and fish could be seen.

He thought it must be his favourite place,
    as he watched two kingfishers enjoy a race.

Then all at once, a tingle in his spine,

Informed him that not everything was fine.

Through grasses and weeds, two BIG BLACK EYES peered.

And though they looked friendly and not at all weird.

They certainly made our poor hero jump,

And he quickly returned to his Mum at the dump.

Perhaps that giant was catching fish?

What a LOT he would need piled up on his dish!

Then Jude remembered his own full plate,

When he scoffed his favourite fish, whitebait,

He did not speak of those eyes near the stream.

Those eyes of the Giant of Pittenweem.

Next day Jude said, "Mum, if you don't mind,
    I don't think I'll go with you down Cove Wynd."

"Are the steps too many for a wee boy to climb?
    We're not in a hurry. We'll take our time."

"No, I really don't want to go down to the pier.
    And I will be happy just to wait here."

"Well, dear if you say so, I won't be long,
    And p'raps one of your friends will come along."

This was a day that Jude did NOT feel brave,

For he dreaded what might be in that dark cave,

Glaring out through the metal barred gate.

He had worked himself into a terrified state.

Saint Fillan had lived in that cave long ago,

Then later, the smugglers had used it to stow,

The contraband goods that came from far places,

Brandy and silks and perfumes and laces.

A Saint or a smuggler, Jude WOULD like to meet,

But he worried about the HAND, EYES and FEET.

When Esther returned, Jude grabbed her hand.
"Let's go home NOW!" was his earnest demand.

That summer was sunny and very hot,
    but they woke one day and it was NOT.
Strange how the weather had suddenly changed!
It seemed as if buildings were re-arranged.

A thick fog hid houses and shops near and far.

Pittenweem was enveloped in the HAAR.

"Oh, let's go for a walk," Jude heard his Mum say,
        "It's quiet and mysterious today.
        Perhaps we will come across something new.
        Now hurry up, Jude! Come along do!"

But Jude was unwilling and quite defiant,
        for he feared his Mum might meet the Giant.

"But the mist makes all things look enchanted
        and perhaps we will find that our wishes are
        granted!"

So Jude agreed and they had not gone far
        before Esther produced a chocolate bar.

Softly stepping down steep Water Wynd,
        no harbour ahead and no High Street behind.

Enclosed in a silent world of their own,

No voices, no cars, all the birds were flown.

"I do really love it, Mum. Now I am out.
        It's so terribly quiet I want to SHOUT"

Then Jude caught a glimpse, but he did not stare.

A massive EAR with a lot of HAIR appeared through the
        branches of a tree, but it was very difficult to see,
        for nothing was sure in that dense milky fog.

A house might be a horse or a cat a dog.

At the swimming pool, Jude loved to dig ditches,

While Esther sat counting her difficult stitches.

All at once, poor Jude leapt as though shot by a gun,

For a great big SOMEONE lay in the sun.

Just at first it was a terrible shock,
      to discover those knees behind the rock,

For these were enormous KNOBBLY knees,

Enough to cause the blood to freeze of a boy less
      valiant than our friend.

But he was a lad that could pretend,

So he quickly looked the other way,

Wondering what he was going to say to protect his
      Mother from this sight,

Which might give her such a terrible fright.

He'd never been SURE what he'd seen in the past,

But now he was convinced at last.

Brave Jude made not a gasp or scream at sight of the
      GIANT OF PITTENWEEM.

But he went back and sat where his Mum was sitting,

And quietly watched her do her knitting.

"I think you must be a tired little lad,
      Let's go home now and make tea for your Dad.".

"Why don't we walk past your favourite shop?
And if you are good we will make a stop."
As it was a hot day in Pittenweem,
Esther bought Jude a delicious ice-cream,
Saying she'd like a shop like that herself,
With jars of sweeties on every shelf.
Outside the shop stood a monster cone.
But it was not real, it was hard as stone.
It was the right size, but it could never please
The owner of those knobbly knees.
What a shame that big man could only dream
Of enjoying the pleasure of ice cream.

While fishermen fished for silver fish and Jude ate
strawberries from a dish, the weather changed
from sun to gloom.

And it became dark in the sitting room.

His Mother frowned and sadly said,

"I'm afraid there's bad weather up ahead.
Tonight there is an eclipse of the moon
and that means storms are coming soon.

Rain clouds are blowing in from the West.
And look how each wave has a little white crest."

In the High Street, no shoppers could be found
and large rain drops bounced on the dusty ground.
Great lightning flashes brightened the sky
and thunder booms made babies cry.

The clouds crowded close and were inky black.

The waves hit the pier with a mighty WHACK.

The wind got wilder and louder and stronger.

Surely this storm could not last much longer!

Jude pressed his nose to the cold window pane.

Would he EVER play down on the beach again?

But the Giant was enjoying all that he saw,
As he lazily leaned against North Berwick Law.

The gale-force wind was terrifying,
    shouting and roaring and gasping and sighing,

Rushing round corners and squeezing thro' gaps
    and scattering seagulls like paper scraps.

And little boys' caps flew out of sight,
    and girls clutched their skirts with all their might,

And mothers grabbed washing down off the line,
    and a poor tethered dog started to whine.

And a galloping cat performed a stunt,
    when its back legs went faster than its front.

No one could remember a storm so bad,
Though Auld Wullie said aye, when he was a lad,
The force of storms was VERY MUCH more,
But who would believe a man of four score?

The waves were hurling up high at the pier
    and the fishermen's wives were filled with fear.

But soon all the boats were hurrying back,

Except for the blue boat of Geordie Jack.

For his heavy catch weighed the boat down low and
    he couldn't make way against that strong blow.

He and his men stood with no sound nor shout,

As those cruel waves tossed their craft about.

They sent off a rocket, brilliant and loud,
    that lit up the underside of a cloud.

When the giant realised their great distress,

He soon dived into that turbulent press.

Through the battering waves those massive arms
ploughed,

To save Geordie's boat the giant had vowed.

His strong stroke soon reached the Isle of May,
    where the poor blue boat helplessly lay.

Its decks were awash and it leaned to the side,

That fine little boat, Geordie's joy and pride.

The Pittenweem Giant with triumphant roar,
    grabbed two ropes in his teeth and headed
    for shore,

Swimming sidestroke in the blustering gale,
    Pittenweem harbour his goal without fail.

Dragging those men in their rescued craft,
    while with joyful relief, each one of them
    laughed.

Four happy wives waited in the wind.

One of them wept and three of them grinned.

They thought this great fellow was just so grand

For bringing their husbands home safely to land.

But the giant did not stop to hear what they'd say,
        for he had disappeared, Cellardyke way.

Please do not believe that he was rude,

Just TOO SHY to accept their gratitude.

Jude witnessed the rescue with excited smiles,
From his secret look-out, high in the tiles.
That the giant was GOOD, he had not guessed.
Such strength and courage! Jude was impressed.
This was a hero who had risked his life
To return each fisherman to his wife.
And the little blue boat was safe as well,
Anchored and rocking gently in the swell,
Where Eider ducks and gulls, their eyes shut fast,
Hid under their wings, 'til the storm was past.

But how would the giant get dry and warm,

After his adventure in the storm?

Who would make sure that he did not catch cold?

And did a giant do what he was told?

Jude knew what his own Mummy would have said,

"A hot milky drink and then off to bed!"

Jude tried to imagine a giant asleep.

How he would have loved to have a quick peep,

At enormous blankets and massive pillows,

As big as the ocean's storm-tossed billows.

A giant's bed must be HUGE, without fail,

And perhaps the cocoa would come in a PAIL.

The sky was clear, the moonlight shone,
The waves had subsided, the storm was gone.
The red-roofed houses were quiet and still,
Lying higgledy-piggledy down the hill.
Jude slept in his bed without any fear,
Knowing the Pittenweem Giant was near.

For though huge and hairy and fierce and gruff,
THE GIANT WAS KIND.
*And that is enough.*

# For the attention of Parents and Grandparents

Pittenweem is a small fishing town in the Kingdom of Fife, on the East Coast of Scotland. It has clung to the hillside above the safe harbour for many hundreds of years, for it was an important port in the eleventh century. Its trade was with Scandinavia and the Hanseatic ports of Northern Europe, and German and Dutch influence is visible in the local architecture, with its cluster of steep, red-tiled roofs. Blankenese is a fishing town on the outskirts of Hamburg in Germany, which has many similarities of construction, although on a larger scale.

No doubt the far travelling seamen also reached the Mediterranean, for many of the local population show traces of Latin in their features and there is a Southern echo in some of their old words and phrases. I was delighted to find that the main town in the Greek island of Naxos bears strong similarities to Pittenweem, with a church crowning the hill and narrow, winding passages, or wynds, leading up and down. Only the flat topped roofs create a very different profile.

While the word 'picturesque' is an obvious word to apply to Pittenweem, it was built with strength, sturdiness and great practical skill. Some of the buildings date from the seventeenth century. That they still stand after three hundred years and still deal successfully with the harsh North Sea weather, (as well as the plentiful run-off water from the slowly rising land behind the town) is a credit to those long-ago builders and plumbers. No doubt there are fine stone-built culverts and passages under the town, yet undiscovered, for we found one below our house very recently.

The town is on two levels and seven narrow wynds connect the High Street with the shore level. Each wynd is unique. Some are enclosed by high walls and houses, while others are more open. Some have flights of steps, some just one or two steps, some have only the sharply rising hill, punishing for those who are unused to ascending such a steep incline. Some wynds curve gently, some have two or three sharp bends. Only one, the Water Wynd is straight. I found it best for returning to the higher level in the days of my strength, when I pushed a pram, sometimes with two small children in it!

Each wynd gives different fascinating views of the sea, as one walks past the charming dwellings. Occasionally there is an unexpected glimpse of a flower-filled garden.

I have travelled those wynds since childhood and know them very well. Nowadays, my grandchildren scamper ahead and wait politely for me, hiding their impatience as best they can.

As far as I know, there is no tradition of a Pittenweem giant, but I have been thinking of the idea for years. My daughter Sarah imagined and drew a giant when she was a child and I have considered writing the story ever since.

He is a benevolent giant and I certainly hope that no small person finds him fearsome.

I would like to think that these illustrations might enrich a wander up and down the wynds of Pittenweem.

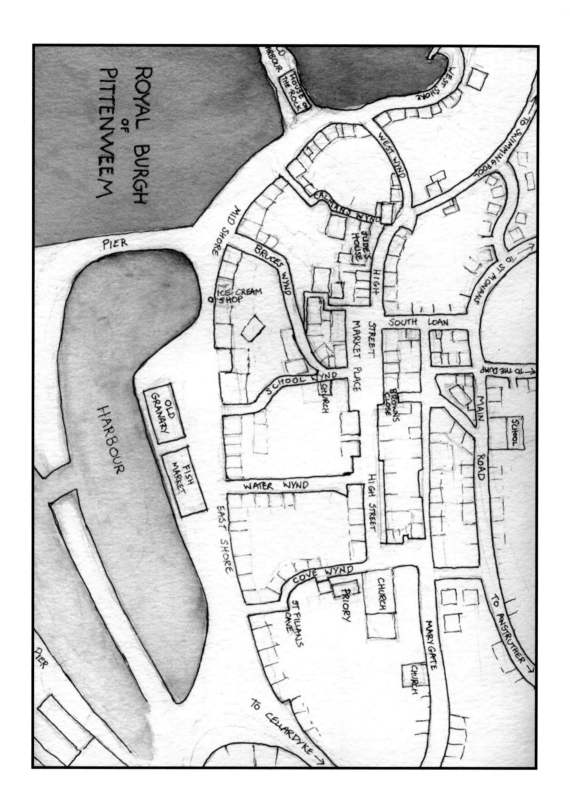